FROG SOUP
and
BUG BREATH

FROG SOUP
and
BUG BREATH

by Janet Adele Bloss

illustrated by Don Robison

Published by Willowisp Press, Inc.
10100 SBF Drive, Pinellas Park, FL 34666

Copyright © 1991 by Willowisp Press, Inc.

Printed in the United States of America

2 4 6 8 10 9 7 5 3

ISBN 0-87406-530-5

To my "little sister," Niky Shumaker, with love

One

The first day of school always made Tiffany nervous. Today was especially scary because this was the first day of middle school. *We sixth-graders will be the babies of the school!* she thought to herself. The seventh and eighth-graders will all seem so much older. She looked up from her bowl of soggy cereal and glanced across the breakfast table at her father.

"Don't worry," Mr. Larson said. "You'll do just fine!"

"I used to be nervous on the first day of school, too," her mother admitted with a smile. "I was shy around the other kids."

Tiffany stared at her mom. It was hard to imagine her mother being nervous or shy. She always had seemed so calm.

Mr. Larson swallowed his last gulp of coffee. "That's right, Tiff," he said. "Your mother was quiet and shy in school. I didn't even notice her until high school when we were in a play together."

Mrs. Larson nodded. "Being in that play gave me a lot of confidence," she said.

Mr. Larson winked. "The play was *Our Town*. It was in that play that I first kissed your mother."

Tiffany wrinkled her nose. "Oh, Dad, how gross!" she exclaimed.

Mrs. Larson's eyes sparkled. "I made a lot of new friends when I joined the Acting Club."

"You were the best actress in the school!" said Mr. Larson. "Suddenly you were popular, and I had to stand in line to get a date! But you finally said yes, and the rest is history." He chuckled and pointed at his wedding ring.

"I guess being in that play changed our lives," added Mrs. Larson. "It was a lot of fun."

"Gee," murmured Tiffany. "All because of a play?"

"That's right," said Mrs. Larson. "Being in that play changed me from a nobody into a somebody." She glanced at her watch. "Ooops! Hurry, Tiff! Let's go! I'll drop you off at school."

As they drove through the town of Madison, Tiffany groaned, "Ugh! Why can't summer vacation be four months long?" Tiffany wished that she could talk to her older sister Carol. *Carol would understand how I feel about going to a new middle school*, Tiffany thought as she stared out the car window.

Suddenly Mrs. Larson said, "It's not the same without Carol, is it? I miss her. She's probably made a lot of new friends in California by now. You know how easily Carol makes friends."

Tiffany nodded. It was as if her mom had read her mind. It seemed to Tiffany that there were about a million miles between Kansas and California.

Mrs. Larson reached out and patted Tiffany

on the shoulder. "Don't be sad, honey," she said. "Out of all the sophomores in the high school, Carol was the one picked to take part in the student exchange program. We should all be proud of her."

"I know," said Tiffany. "But I really miss her."

"So do I," agreed her mom. "But remember, it's just for one school year. And she's staying with a nice family. She's a special girl."

That's right, Tiffany thought to herself. *Carol really is special. That's why I wish she were here. She's so popular, she could give me hints on how to make friends at the new school.*

Mrs. Larson stopped the car in front of Madison Middle School. Tiffany climbed slowly out of the car and waved to her mother. Turning to face the school building, she took a few deep breaths. Groups of students crowded the sidewalk. Sure enough, Tiffany thought they seemed older and more mature than the students in the old elementary school. She felt her stomach flutter at the sight of all those strange faces.

"Get a hold of yourself, Tiffany Larson!" she muttered. "You're such a chicken! Carol's in a new school hundreds of miles away, and you're afraid to go to a new school in your own little town!"

Tiffany was looking around for a face she recognized when she heard someone calling her name. A red-haired girl walked toward her.

"Erin!" Tiffany called to her best friend. "Pretty weird, huh? All these new faces!"

"It sure is. What's your first class?" Erin asked.

"English."

"Mine too!" exclaimed Erin. "We're in the same class!"

The bell rang. The two girls ran into the school and dashed down the hall looking for their homeroom. After what seemed like a hundred announcements in homeroom, Tiffany and Erin wandered around the hallways until they found their English class. Tiffany looked around. With a sigh of relief, she saw a few familiar faces mixed in with all the new ones.

"Welcome to sixth-grade English," said the teacher with a warm smile from the front of the room. "I'm Ms. Carver."

Tiffany found it hard to concentrate on what the teacher was saying. She stared out the window and wished that she were at the swimming pool with her friends.

"We have a fun year ahead of us," the teacher said. "We'll visit the town library. We'll have an author visit the class. We'll write our own stories, and we'll put on a play in October."

Tiffany's ears perked up. She remembered her mother's words at breakfast: *Being in that play gave me a lot of confidence...I made a lot of new friends...Being in that play changed me from a nobody into a somebody.*

Hmm, thought Tiffany. *Maybe this play business is the answer.* She started to pay attention.

"Every October the sixth grade performs a play in front of the whole school," continued Ms. Carver. "The fall play is one of the biggest events of the year at Madison Middle School. We'll spend several weeks rehearsing for the play."

A girl waved her hand in the air.

"Yes?" Ms. Carver called. Then she added, "Tell me your names so I can start to learn all your names."

"When will the tryouts be?" the girl asked. "I'm Heather Truman."

"We'll have tryouts in three weeks, Heather," she said.

"I'm Mike Boyd. What's the play about?" asked a boy from the back row.

"It's a comedy," replied Ms. Carver. "The name of the play is *Frog Soup*."

A gale of laughter burst from the classroom. Tiffany giggled. "Frog soup?" she whispered to Erin. "Mmmmm, tasty!"

"It's a very funny play," explained Ms. Carver. "I encourage all you comedians and jokers to try out. There are two lead roles, one for a girl and one for a boy. They'll play the frog princess and the frog prince. Then there are the minor roles: a dancing mushroom, a fly, several elves, and some others."

Tiffany leaned her chin into her hand, daydreaming about winning the lead role of the princess. *Everyone would know who I am*, she thought. *I'd make new friends, and Mom and Dad would be proud of me! I'd definitely go from being a nobody into being a somebody. Maybe I'd become just as popular as Mom was when she was in the play!*

A wonderful daydream filled Tiffany's head. In the daydream, she stood on stage in the auditorium filled with people. Her family sat in the first row—Mom, Dad, and Carol. Tiffany imagined herself holding a microphone, telling joke after joke, just like a stand-up comedian on TV.

Why do cows wear bells? Tiffany asked in her daydream. *Because their horns don't work!*

In Tiffany's daydream, hundreds of people roared with laughter as she told her jokes. *Who's that girl?* they asked each other. *Don't you know? She's Tiffany Larson*, came the answer.

She's new here, a sixth-grader. She's really popular...and funny!

Tiffany sighed as the wonderful daydream rolled through her head like a movie. But then a sudden thought came into Tiffany's head. It exploded her golden daydream just like a popped balloon.

"Gina," Tiffany whispered under her breath. Suddenly Tiffany didn't feel so hopeful. After all, Gina Gold always got the lead in every class play. Ever since first grade, it was always Gina who stood on center stage. It was always Gina who told the jokes and made the whole class crack up. Tiffany leaned her head on her hand and groaned.

Tiffany looked at the front of the room. "I'll put a sign-up sheet on the bulletin board for those of you who would like to be in the fall play," Ms. Carver was saying.

Tiffany turned to Erin. "Why does she bother to put up a sign-up sheet?" she asked. "No one stands a chance with Gina around. She always gets the best part."

Erin leaned across the aisle. "Didn't you know?" she whispered.

"Know what?" asked Tiffany.

"Gina moved to Washington over the summer. Her dad got a job there."

"What?" Tiffany's brown eyes widened with surprise. "Y-you mean, Gina's not here anymore?"

Erin shook her head.

This was too good to be true! Maybe her daydream had some life in it after all. "I can do it," Tiffany muttered under her breath. "I'll get the part of the frog princess."

"It's a comedy, remember," Erin said.

"I know. I'm funny," Tiffany answered. "And I'll practice telling jokes so I'm even funnier! I'll prove to everybody that I'm funny enough to get the lead in the play!"

The bell rang and almost everyone jumped up and raced to the bulletin board. "Anyone have a pencil I can borrow?" Tiffany shouted.

A hand with red polished nails appeared out of the crowd. Handing a pencil to Tiffany, Ms. Carver said, "Here you go,...uh...Kimberley?"

"My name's Tiffany. Tiffany Larson."

"Sorry," Ms. Carver apologized with a smile. "It'll take me a few days to learn everyone's name. Hmmmm," Ms Carver added with a thoughtful look. "Are you Carol Larson's sister?"

"Uh huh," Tiffany answered.

"Isn't Carol in high school now? Wasn't she the student chosen for the exchange program?" asked Ms. Carver.

Tiffany nodded.

"I remember your sister," the teacher said. "Carol was a good student and a member of the debate team."

Everyone knows Carol, thought Tiffany. *I'm a nobody. But when I get the star role in this play, everyone will know who I am. I'll be a somebody!*

When Tiffany finally got to the front of the sign-up line, she saw 18 names already on the list. She slowly wrote her name and gave the pencil back to the teacher. When Tiffany walked into the hall, she found Erin waiting for her.

"Gee," Tiffany said. "I guess it's going to be harder than I thought to get the lead. There were already 18 names on the list before me. I think you're the only person in the whole class who's not signing up."

"I'd be too nervous." Erin answered. "Do you think you can do it?"

"I have to do it!" Tiffany said. "If I get the starring role in the play, then I'll be popular and have loads of friends."

Tiffany noticed that Erin looked a little unhappy. "Well, it *is* important to have friends, you know."

"You've got me. I'm your friend, aren't I?" Erin answered. "What's wrong with me?"

Tiffany looked at Erin. "Uh, nothing's wrong with you. I didn't mean that. I just mean I want to get the lead role in the play so that people will know who I am, that's all."

"Oh."

"And the first thing I have to do is show Ms. Carver that I'm the funniest kid in the sixth grade. Once she sees how funny I am, I'll get the lead role in Frog Soup for sure!"

"But how are you going to get her to notice how funny you are?"

Tiffany paused in the hallway for a moment. "I don't know yet," she said. "But I'll think of something. It's the best way to stop being a nobody!"

Suddenly something on the bulletin board in the hall caught Tiffany's eye. It was a sign that said:

GO BULLDOGS!!!
6th GRADE FOOTBALL TEAM TRYOUTS
TODAY (THURSDAY) AFTER SCHOOL
ON THE FOOTBALL FIELD.
SEE COACH MUNKLE.

Erin looked at Tiffany and said, "Uh-oh. I hope you're not thinking what I think you're thinking!"

Tiffany had a funny little smile on her face. "Well, it would get everybody's attention."

Erin gasped. "Tiffany!" she exclaimed. "You're not really seriously thinking about... You're a... And besides, you don't even like..."

"Football?" asked Tiffany with a wink. "Why not? Have you seen some of the wimpy guys in our class? I'll bet I can play football better than some of them! I mean, all you do is run around with the ball and not let anyone catch you, right? There's nothing more to it!"

"I don't know," Erin answered.

Tiffany tucked her books under her arm like a football and took off down the hall looking for her next class. "See you at lunch!" she called back over her shoulder.

Two

The last bell of the day rang. Tiffany found herself at her locker surrounded by sixth-grade girls. Some of them were from the old elementary school. Others were new faces.

"You're not really going out for the boys' football team, are you?" asked Heather Truman.

"They'll *kill* you!" exclaimed Erin.

"Where will you take a shower?" asked Allison Bosley. "You won't have to go in the boys' locker room, will you?"

"You won't have to wear, you know, boys' underwear, will you?" asked Heather giggling.

"What if they knock your teeth out?" asked Susie Kurtz. "I heard that all football players have fake teeth because they get them knocked out playing football."

Tiffany gulped. "They do?" she asked, shutting her locker door. "I just got my braces off." Then, with a brave smile on her face, she said, "Stand back, girls. I'm going to be the best half-quarter-tackle-back this school has ever seen!"

"But Tiffany, you don't know a thing about football," Erin reminded her.

"I'll learn," Tiffany said loudly. Leaning close to Erin, she whispered, "I'm trying to get Ms. Carver's attention. When she hears about this, I'll get the part in Frog Soup for sure! Then I won't be a nobody in this school. I'll be popular like my Mom was...and like my sister Carol is."

Tiffany grabbed her gym bag. She headed for the girls' locker room with Erin. Tiffany changed into shorts and a T-shirt. Erin said, "I'll bet no one else going out for the football team is wearing a bra with little pink roses on it."

They both laughed. Tiffany pulled a brush through her short black hair, then put on some strawberry lip gloss. "I'll probably be the only one wearing lip gloss, too," she said. "Okay! I'm ready now!"

Erin shook her head as she followed Tiffany from the locker room. They walked through the gym, then outside onto the football field. Tiffany felt her heart quake when she saw boys running onto the field, yelling. Most of them were from the old elementary school. And they looked huge. They clapped each other on the back and punched each other in the shoulders.

"If anyone punches me, I'll get my parents to sue them," Tiffany muttered under her breath.

Erin sat on the first row of bleachers "Good luck," she said to Tiffany. "I think you're going to need it."

"Here goes nothing," said Tiffany as she ran onto the field. She headed for the tall man with a silver whistle in his hand. Tiffany smiled nervously. "Hello, Coach Munkle," she said. "Nice day for a touchdown, huh?"

Coach Munkle raised his eyebrows. "The cheerleaders are practicing in the gym," he said.

"Yes, thank you, sir," Tiffany said. "I know. I'm going out for the football team." Tiffany stood as tall as she could, trying to look tough. But her legs and shoulders felt as if they were made out of marshmallows. When someone bumped into her, Tiffany turned to see Bart Henson, who looked like the biggest guy in the sixth grade.

"Come on!" snorted Bart. "You're going out for the team? Don't make me laugh!"

But Tiffany remembered that was exactly what she *wanted* everyone to do. She wanted them to laugh. After all, wasn't she trying to prove she was funny? Didn't she want to get the lead role in a comedy?

She was about to say something mean back to Bart when she saw a girl jogging across the football field. The girl came closer. Tiffany didn't know her. Her hair was pulled back in a ponytail.

"Hi, Coach Munkle," she said. "I'm Wendy Hall. I'd like to go out for the team. I played half-back on the Little Elks team this summer. I scored eleven touchdowns in eight games."

The whistle dropped out of the coach's mouth.

"I run three miles a day, too," she added.

Tiffany stared in shock. "Are you serious?" she asked.

"Sure, I'm serious," answered Wendy. She stood with her hands on her hips.

Tiffany leaned closer. "Do you understand how to play?" she asked. "Isn't this the silliest game in the world?"

"It's not silly," Wendy answered. "I like football. It's easy to understand. You try to score more touchdowns than the other team."

"Easy?" Tiffany said as she rolled her eyes. "Where's the free throw line? Where's first base?"

The boys who had gathered around the two girls all laughed. The coach blew his whistle and shouted, "Okay guys...uhhh, and girls, let's get started."

Tiffany turned to Coach Munkle. "I definitely don't want anyone to knock my teeth out. Mom and Dad paid a fortune for my braces. My parents will kill me if anything happens to my teeth."

Coach Munkle took off his hat. "Are you sure you want to try out for the team?" he asked.

"Yes!" Tiffany exclaimed.

The coach shrugged his shoulders. Then he blew his whistle and shouted, "Okay. We'll do the tires first," he said.

"Tires?" Tiffany muttered. She watched as Wendy and all the boys ran, whooping and hollering, over to two lines of car tires lying side-by-side across the ground. Ben Poston stepped into one tire, then another, running as fast as he could. The other guys shouted encouragement as Ben's legs pumped up and down like pistons. Wendy followed him, stepping quickly from one tire to another.

"Let's go, Tiff," growled Bart. "You're up next."

Tiffany glanced over at the bleachers. Erin sat with her hands covering her eyes. Heather, Susie, and Arlene had joined Erin in the bleachers. Big smiles stretched across their faces as Tiffany waved at them.

All right! It's working, Tiffany thought. *I'm getting everyone's attention. Pretty soon everyone will know I'm the craziest girl in the school!*

"Move it!" growled Bart, giving Tiffany a nudge.

Tiffany whirled around. "Quit shoving!" she squealed.

She walked carefully up to the tires and looked down at them. She lifted her foot carefully into one, then the other. She hopped back and forth, trying to run the way Ben and Wendy did. But Tiffany looked as if she was playing hopscotch. As she moved, lifting her legs high enough to get over the tires, she felt as if her thighs were going to drop off. Suddenly her heel hit the side of a tire, and she fell. Bart Henson, who had been following, rolled on top of her. Then Mike Boyd dropped on top of him. And Scott Aaron fell on all of them.

"Owww!" howled Tiffany. "Get off! Your foot's

on my face! Careful! Watch my teeth!"

Coach Munkle walked over to the wriggling pile of bodies on the tires. Reaching down, he took Tiffany's hand and pulled her up. Tiffany felt her teeth to make sure they were all still there.

"Have you had enough?" the coach asked with a sigh.

Tiffany straightened her T-shirt. "Well, maybe this isn't the right sport for me," she admitted. "Maybe I'll try something with less contact."

"Try Ping-Pong," Bart growled. All the boys began laughing.

Wendy turned to Tiffany. "Will you get out of here?" she hissed. "Don't spoil it for me. I'm a good player, and I really want to be on the team. I just hope they give me a chance after the way you messed up!"

Tiffany noticed that the group in the bleachers had grown. There must have been 30 boys and girls laughing as if they'd never seen anything so funny.

So far, so good! Tiffany thought as she walked off the field toward the bleachers. She tried to ignore Wendy's frown. She gave the crowd a thumbs-up.

"Gosh," exclaimed Erin. "I can't believe you did that, Tiff! What'll you think of next?"

Tiffany smiled mysteriously. "Oh, I just might have a little something up my sleeve," she answered. "Wait until tomorrow. You'll see!"

Three

TODAY!

TIFFANY LARSON

will eat a

crunchy, gooey, yucky

bug!

in the parking lot after school

FREE!!!!!

"I saw the sign in the girls' locker room!" screamed Erin, waiting beside Tiffany's locker the next morning. "It's a joke, right? You wouldn't really eat a bug, would you?"

Tiffany shot a glance around the hall to see if

anyone was listening. Students hurried by. "I don't know if it's a joke or not," she whispered. "I don't know if I'm going to go through with it."

"Well, why'd you put the sign up?" Erin asked.

"It's a publicity stunt," Tiffany answered. "I put signs up all over school. I even put one up in English class. Ms. Carver will notice me now, for sure. She'll see how crazy I am and give me the lead in the play. Then my life will change and I'll be popular. If it worked for Mom, it'll work for me."

"Did your mom have to eat a bug?" asked Erin.

"Well...no. But *Frog Soup* is a comedy, right? And what's funnier than someone eating a bug?"

Erin looked a little green. "I don't know, Tiff. It's not so funny for the person who has to eat the bug, is it?"

The corners of Tiffany's mouth tugged downward. She swallowed. "Maybe you're right."

But just then, Bart Henson walked by Tiffany's locker. He stopped and said, "Eat a bug? Someone's going to eat a bug?"

"I-I—" Tiffany stuttered.

"No way!" said Bart. "The only person crazy enough to eat a bug is Gina Gold. And she moved away. Too bad. She was really nuts!"

Tiffany frowned.

Mike Boyd and Heather Truman joined the group. "Are you Tiffany Larson?" Mike asked.

Tiffany nodded.

"I saw your sign," said Mike. "About eating the bug."

"What about it?" Tiffany asked.

"You're only going to eat one bug? *Anybody* can eat one bug by accident, like if one flew into your glass or got stuck on your peanut butter, and you ate it without knowing it."

"So?"

"So why don't you eat two bugs?"

"Two bugs?" Tiffany said in a small voice, looking around at the crowd, which had grown to more than 20 people.

"I'll bet you're going to eat some puny, little bug," continued Mike. "Big deal. If you were really crazy, you'd eat a giant bug—one with wings."

"Eat a bug with big eyeballs, too!" demanded Allison Bosley, who had joined the group. "If you're not chicken."

Tiffany slammed her locker shut. "Okay! Okay! I'll do it! I'll eat two bugs after school," she announced. "Two bugs with wings and also big eyeballs."

"*And* big, fat, wiggly legs?" asked Bart. "Gina Gold would do it."

"And long feelers?" asked another person.

Tiffany swallowed. She said slowly, "Yes. I, Tiffany Larson, will eat two bugs with wings, big eyeballs, wiggly legs, and feelers."

"And sharp pincers?" another kid yelled.

"And pincers," Tiffany said. "But that's all!"

All the kids cheered and clapped. Erin wrinkled her nose. Tiffany looked around with a smile on her face. She waved to the crowd. "Thank you, thank you," she said, bowing.

"Can I catch the bugs for you?" asked Mike Boyd. "I've seen some big, fat ones by the drinking fountain outside."

Tiffany nodded. "Sure, you bring the bugs," she said. "I'll bring my appetite." Tiffany slowly licked her lips. "Bugs, yum!" she exclaimed. Some people in the crowd made gagging noises. Then Tiffany marched off through the crowd to homeroom with Erin right behind her.

"Are you really going to do it?" whispered Erin. "I don't think it's a very good idea."

"I've *got* to do it now," Tiffany groaned. "I'll never be popular if everyone thinks I'm a liar and a chicken. I wasn't going to do it until they started talking about how Gina would have done it. And then just to show them, I said I'd do it. So now I have to do it!"

Tiffany had a hard time paying attention in class the whole morning. No matter how hard she tried to think about schoolwork, all she could see in front of her eyes were shiny, black bugs, wriggling and twitching. Her stomach kept doing flip-flops through English class when she was supposed to be reading American poetry. And she could barely look at her math problems because when she squinted her eyes and looked at the little black figures in her book, they looked like—guess what.

The only good thing was between classes when she passed people in the halls. She saw a seventh-grader point and whisper, "That's the girl who's going to eat the bugs!" Tiffany had to keep reminding herself why she was going through with it. *I'm doing it because it will get me the lead in the play for sure*, she thought. *Pretty soon every kid in this school will know who I am!*

At lunch Erin offered Tiffany half of her peanut butter sandwich. "You'd better eat extra food," Erin said. "You need to coat your stomach before you...before you.... I can't say it!"

"Eat the bugs," Tiffany said bravely.

"Are you really going to do it?" asked Arlene Dobbs, joining their table.

Tiffany nodded. "Sure," she said, loud enough for people at the other tables to hear. "A bug a day keeps the doctor away."

Several people put down their lunches.

"Haven't you heard about the new bug-a-day diet?" Tiffany continued. "It's cholesterol-free and high in fiber."

A girl at the end of their table got up and walked away.

"Enough is enough," whispered Erin.

"But what if you eat a mother bug, and it has babies in your stomach?" asked Arlene. "What if your stomach fills up with hundreds of bugs? What if they start crawling out your nose and eyes and ears while you're asleep?"

It was Tiffany's turn to feel sick. "Let's not talk about it anymore, okay?" she said and took a sip from her milk. Suddenly, she didn't feel much like eating.

The hours of the afternoon went by too slow

and too fast. Tiffany wanted to hurry up and get it over with. But she also wanted the clock to stop so that she would never have to eat the bugs. *Maybe we'll have a tornado or a flash flood, and everyone will forget about me eating bugs*, she hoped. But looking out the window in study hall, Tiffany saw that the sun was shining brightly.

When the last bell of the day rang, Tiffany found Erin waiting at her locker with a grim look on her face. "You don't have to go through with it," Erin whispered. "Everyone knows you're funny enough."

Before Tiffany could answer, Bart Henson ran by and shouted, "See you in the parking lot, Tiff. You're as crazy as Gina Gold!"

"I'm crazier!" Tiffany shouted back. "Just wait!" Then she said to Erin, "Come on. I might as well get this over with. Keep reminding me how popular I'm going to be."

"I asked the school nurse if it could hurt you to eat bugs," said Erin.

"What'd she say?"

"She said it wouldn't be dangerous at all. She says in some places bugs are a delicacy."

"Well, that's a relief," answered Tiffany.

Tiffany heard the crowd in the parking lot even before she got there. They were chanting her name as if she were a rock star.

"Tiff-a-ny! Tiff-a-ny! Tiff-a-ny!"

"If my parents could see me now," she told Erin, "they'd probably ground me forever. I don't think they'd want their daughter eating bugs in public...or in private."

"Here she comes!" someone called as Tiffany turned the corner. A cheer went up.

"Will she really do it?"

"Where are the bugs? Wow! They're huge!"

"Ooooo gross!"

The crowd parted to let Tiffany through. She looked to see if Ms. Carver was there, but the English teacher was nowhere in sight. Disappointed, Tiffany stopped beside Mike. He pulled a plastic sandwich bag from his pocket.

"These were the biggest bugs I could find," he

announced. He held the bag up for the crowd of at least a hundred kids to see. The crowd gasped.

Tiffany felt her stomach lurch when she saw the two black beetles in the bag. Their legs scraped at the side of the bag as they struggled to escape. *I know you're scared, bugs*, thought Tiffany. *But not as scared as I am.*

For a moment Tiffany thought that she might faint. Her skin got cold and clammy, and her head felt light. She looked around at all of the kids who were watching her. Some were from the old elementary school. Others were new kids she'd never met.

Every one of them will know me now if I go ahead and eat the bugs, Tiffany told herself. *I'll definitely be the funniest kid in the whole class. They'll have to give me the lead role in the play!*

Tiffany gazed around the crowd. They were still chanting her name. *But if I back out now*, she thought, *I'll be a nobody again. I'll be worse than a nobody. I'll be famous as the biggest liar in the sixth grade.*

Forcing a smile, Tiffany asked, "Does anyone have a cracker? I like to eat my beetles in a little sandwich. Don't you?"

Nervous laughter rippled through the crowd. Arlene opened her lunch box and took out some crackers. She handed them to Tiffany. Tiffany took one last look around at all the people who had come to watch her. She took a deep breath as Mike gave her the plastic bag.

Tiffany reached into the bag for the first beetle. She felt the hard shell as she placed the beetle between the crackers. That was better. She could barely see them.

Don't think about it, don't think about it, she told herself. *Think about getting the lead in the play. Think about being more popular than Gina Gold.*

Tiffany shut her eyes tightly. She heard the crowd gasping and groaning. She felt her mouth chewing, and she felt her throat swallowing. Twice.

And when she opened her eyes again, there

were no bugs in the plastic bag, and the crowd of kids was going wild. They had rushed up to her and were shouting and cheering and slapping her on the back. Two boys lifted her on their shoulders and carried her around.

"Look out!" someone shouted. "She's going to barf!"

The crowd moved away. But Tiffany brushed a hand across her mouth and said in a weak voice, "Mmmm, crunchy."

"Three cheers for Bug Breath!" Mike Boyd yelled. "Hip! Hip! Hooray!" echoed the crowd.

"What did it taste like?" asked Erin, handing her a plastic cup of water.

"Well," said Tiffany, "I don't know. I guess it tasted...buggy!"

The crowd laughed some more. Finally after a lot more cheering and yelling, the boys let Tiffany down, and she hurried away from school with Erin.

"Well, was it worth it?" Erin asked when they stopped in front of Tiffany's house.

"Yes, a million times yes!" answered Tiffany, chewing on three pieces of gum to get rid of the buggy taste. "Just wait until Ms. Carver hears about it. I probably won't even have to try out for *Frog Soup* now. She'll be begging me to play the princess! Or *bugging* me to play the princess!"

"Very funny," Erin said shaking her head. "I don't know, Tiff," she answered. "Eating those bugs was really gross. I think you went too far this time."

"What do you mean?" asked Tiffany. "Eating bugs won't hurt me, and now every kid in the school will know who I am by Monday morning."

"Maybe, but I still think you went too far. I don't know if being popular is worth eating bugs."

"You just don't understand! I need to be popular!" Tiffany answered as Erin started for home. But Erin didn't answer.

That night at dinner, Tiffany listened as her mother read a letter from Carol. "She says she's made a lot of new friends. Isn't that wonderful?"

Carol probably didn't have to eat a bug to make new friends, decided Tiffany. "Yeah, Mom, that's nice," she said.

"What's wrong, honey?" her mom asked. "You've hardly eaten a thing. I thought you loved spaghetti with mushrooms."

Tiffany stared down at her plate. "It's the mushrooms," she moaned. "They look like...like bugs."

Her parents laughed. "Tiffany, you have a wild imagination!" her father said. "Why would anyone eat a bug?"

"I don't know," Tiffany muttered. "To be popular?"

Her dad smiled. "Tiff! What will you think of next?"

"Could I be excused?" Tiffany asked. "I'm not hungry."

Four

Monday morning came. After chewing gum for what seemed like all weekend, Tiffany finally had the taste of bugs out of her mouth. As she walked through the hall to her locker, she wondered how the kids would act towards her. *Will they treat me like the same old nobody*, she asked herself, *or will I be a somebody?*

Several kids she didn't know smiled or waved at her, and a few gave her the thumbs-up. When Tiffany walked into English class, she saw Heather Truman and Mike Boyd standing together. They both smiled—the kind of smiles that the kids used to smile at Gina Gold, Tiffany decided proudly.

The students rushed to their seats as the

final bell rang. Ms. Carver stood in front of the room. Tiffany glanced at the *Frog Soup* sign-up sheet on the bulletin board. Tryouts are coming up, she reminded herself. *Hmm, I don't have much time to show Ms. Carver how funny I am. I sure wish she would have seen me eat the bugs. I've got to do something...fast!*

"Today we've got a special project," announced Ms. Carver. "Some of you actors will get a chance to show off your talent."

Tiffany's ears perked up.

"As you know, this is the week of the Madison Bulldogs' first football game of the season, against the Spring Valley Warriors. We all want to support the school, don't we?"

"Yes!" shouted the class.

"Well, there's going to be a pep rally Wednesday in the auditorium. Each class—the sixth, seventh, and eighth—will put on a short skit. This English class has been chosen to represent the sixth grade. Who'd like to volunteer for our class's skit? We need three people."

Tiffany's hand shot into the air. Lots of other hands joined hers, waving madly. *Me, me, me,* Tiffany pleaded silently. *Please choose me!*

Ms. Carver pointed and said, "Heather Truman, Mike Boyd, and..."

Tiffany flapped her arm frantically.

"Tiffany Larson."

"Yippee!" Tiffany whispered under her breath. She turned to Erin and added, "Now I'll get to prove what a good actor I am. I'll show her how funny I can be."

"Practice will be today after school in this room," said the teacher.

For the rest of the day, Tiffany felt as if she were floating on a cloud. *I can't believe it,* she told herself. *I'm going to be in a skit in front of the whole school!*

When the final bell of the day rang, she hurried to her English classroom. Ms. Carver, Mike Boyd, and Heather Truman were waiting there. Handing a piece of paper to Tiffany, Ms. Carver said, "Here's your script. You'll play the part of the Spring Valley Warrior. Mike's the Madison Bulldog and Heather's the announcer."

"You're the one who gets killed in the skit," Mike said with a grin.

Tiffany frowned as she read over her part. The biggest thing she did was fall down dead after Mike the Bulldog growled at her a few times. "Is this all?" asked Tiffany. "Don't I get to say anything? I mean, it's such a teeny part."

Ms. Carver smiled. "There's no such thing as a small part," she said. "All parts are important."

I think some parts are more important than other parts, thought Tiffany, grumping.

They started rehearsing. Heather read her lines like an announcer at a game. Tiffany hopped around like an Indian warrior. Mike growled and rushed at her. He pretended to knock her with his arm. Tiffany read her script. It said:

Warrior: Fall down and lie still.

Tiffany sank to the floor. It smelled like hundreds of shoes and tons of dust. "Aw-aw-aw-

CHOOOOO!" she sneezed.

"Don't sneeze when we give the skit at the rally," Heather warned. "Dead people don't sneeze. It's a medical fact."

Over and over again they practiced their parts. Tiffany hopped and fell and tried not to sneeze. As she lay on the dusty floor, she kept reminding herself that all great actors probably started their careers in the same way. Everyone had to start at the bottom.

You can't get much lower than this, she told herself as she lay on the floor, staring at a thumbtack and a dust ball.

"Good," said Ms. Carver finally. "I think you're ready for the pep rally."

As soon as Tiffany got home, she went up to her room. She practiced moaning and falling to the floor. "If I have to die, I might as well do it with style," she muttered.

Suddenly, her bedroom door opened, and her mother popped her head in. She stared at Tiffany lying on the floor. "Honey, are you all right?"

she asked.

Tiffany jumped to her feet. "I'm okay, Mom," she answered. "I'm practicing for a play. I'm going to act in front of the whole school!"

"That's wonderful!"

"Well," said Tiffany. "It's more like a little skit, not a real play."

"I'm sure you'll do fine. Carol was in a class play when she was your age. She played the part of Cinderella."

Tiffany thought that playing Cinderella sounded a lot better than playing a dead Indian. But then she reminded herself that this skit was just a first step to larger things—*Frog Soup!*

"Watch me, Mom. Here's my part!" Tiffany moaned dramatically and placed the back of her hand against her forehead. She twirled, waved her arms, stumbled, and fell in a heap on the floor. "I'm dead, Mom," she said. "Do I look dead?"

"You sure do."

Tiffany heard the front door open. "That must be Dad," she said, jumping up and running to the front door. "Dad! Hey, Dad!" Tiffany cried. "I have a part in a school skit. Want to see me practice?"

As her father watched with wide eyes, she moaned loudly and stumbled out the front door. She crashed to the ground into a large clump of chrysanthemums.

* * * * * * * * * *

Tiffany felt uneasy on Wednesday afternoon even though she had practiced her part about a thousand times. The students filed into the auditorium. Tiffany sat in the middle of the front row between Mike and Heather. They waited nervously for the seventh and eighth-graders to do their skits.

At last the time came for the sixth-graders to perform. Ms. Carver announced their skit to the students in the packed auditorium and Tiffany's heart started to beat faster. The three actors walked up on the stage to the sound of clapping.

From memory, Heather spoke her lines. "Soon the mighty Bulldogs will meet the Warriors in a battle to the death. The ferocious Bulldogs will charge onto the field in a blaze of courage and strength."

Mike, wearing a Bulldog football helmet, stomped across the stage with a fierce look on his face. Growling, snarling and barking, he sidestepped a group of chairs as if they were other football players.

Heather continued in her announcer's voice as Mike jumped around. Finally she said, "It will be a mighty battle. But in the end, we all know who is going to win! The Bulldogs will stomp the Warriors!"

Hearing her cue, Tiffany hopped onto the stage wearing Indian feathers, and faced Mike. Suddenly, she felt a strange, powerful wave of excitement pass through her as she realized the whole school was watching her. Mike growled and pretended to push Tiffany. This was her cue to die.

Tiffany hopped. She moaned. She howled and shrieked in agony as she twirled around and around. She flapped her arms and waved her hands. She fell to one knee. But then, using all the strength of a mortally wounded Indian, she dragged herself to her feet and stumbled across the stage. She fell again, knocking over some wooden chairs and sending them flying all over the stage.

"Oh, I'm dying!" she shrieked. Reaching out, she grabbed for Heather's ankle.

"Let go!" squealed Heather.

"Awwwwrk!" Tiffany squawked. As Heather tried to walk away, she dragged the moaning Tiffany across the stage. Tiffany wailed, then finally let go. She lay in the center of the stage, kicking her feet into the air and making horrible screeching sounds as she died. Mike stood staring at her, having forgotten all his lines.

The auditorium filled with cheering and laughing. With one final, terrible shudder, the

Indian died. Tiffany lay motionless on the stage. Mike and Heather looked as if they didn't know what to do. Tiffany opened one eye and saw the whole student body standing and cheering.

Jumping to her feet, she took off her feather headdress and waved it around, yelling, "Go Bulldogs! Stomp the Warriors!"

After leading the crowd in this cheer for a few minutes, while Mike and Heather just gaped, Tiffany waved and ran off the stage. She looked back and saw the principal trying to calm the students. She was a star! She had proved it to everyone!

But when she turned around, she was face to face with Mike and Heather. "You wrecked everything!" Heather cried with tears in her eyes.

"Why did you add all that other stuff?" demanded Mike. "That wasn't in the script!"

"I-I just wanted to make it more interesting," Tiffany protested. "They loved it! Can't you hear them?"

Tiffany heard the sound of high heels tap-

ping across the floor. Ms. Carver appeared, frowning.

"She ruined everything!" Heather wailed.

"You didn't follow your script, Tiffany," said the teacher. "That's not how we practiced it." She seemed to be waiting for an answer.

"I-I..." But Tiffany couldn't say anything. It didn't seem fair. Why was everyone so mad? Didn't they hear the students going wild— laughing and screaming and shouting?

Ms. Carver turned and walked away without another word. Tiffany found herself staring into the angry eyes of Mike and Heather. Tiffany plucked a feather from her hair and turned away. *They're just jealous because I stole the show and the crowd loved me*, she thought.

I'll just have to be funnier, Tiffany decided. *No one will stay mad at me if I make them laugh.*

Five

Walking into the school building the next day, lots of kids said hi and congratulated Tiffany on her skit performance.

"Hey! It's the dying Indian!" the kids shouted.

But Tiffany was a little bit afraid to face Mike and Heather. She decided that the best way to get them to like her again was to try out some of her best new jokes on them.

"Knock, knock," Tiffany asked before English class, walking up to them with a smile.

"Okay. Who's there?" asked Mike.

"Danielle," said Tiffany.

"Danielle who?" Heather asked.

Tiffany covered her ears with her hands. "Danielle so loud," she said, "I can hear you!"

Mike and Heather laughed. Tiffany sighed with relief. *I hope they're not mad at me anymore*, she thought to herself, *but it's good to keep reminding them how funny I am.*

"Class," said Ms. Carver, "today we're going up to the library. Ms. Beanell, the librarian, is going to explain the new computerized library system to us. I want you all to listen carefully to what Ms. Beanell has to say."

"Ms. Beanpole," Tiffany whispered.

Giggles erupted in the classroom. Ms. Carver glanced across the room. The students became quiet. Then the class followed her through the halls and upstairs to the library. Tiffany pretended that she had caught her ankle in a bear trap. She hobbled along, bobbing up and down. The other students snorted with laughter.

"Good morning, Ms. Beanell," said Ms. Carver as she entered the library. The librarian smiled cheerfully at the group. She asked them to sit at the library tables.

Ms. Carver turned to her students. "I know

you all will be good," she said. "I'm sure that Ms. Beanell has a lot of information to share with you. So listen carefully. I'll be back in an hour."

When Ms. Carver had left, Ms. Beanell said, "We have three computer terminals in the library. Gather around and I'll show you how to use them." Ms. Beanell sat down at the computer table, and the class crowded around her.

"You press the control key and the display key," Ms. Beanell explained.

Tiffany had snuck around behind the librarian. When she had gotten the attention of some of her classmates, Tiffany pushed her lips into the shape of a fish mouth. Her eyes bulged. She wiggled her fingers under her chin like fins. All the students' eyes turned from Ms. Beanell to watch Tiffany. She did her imitation of a cross-eyed goldfish. Quiet laughter rippled through the group.

"Why did the cross-eyed teacher have to leave school?" whispered Tiffany.

"Why?" Arlene whispered back.

"Because he couldn't control his pupils!" Tiffany answered. The students choked back their laughter.

"If you have trouble looking for a book," explained Ms. Beanell, "just press the help key."

Tiffany mouthed the librarian's words behind her back. She squinted her eyes and mashed her nose up against her face. She chattered her teeth, doing her crazed chipmunk imitation. Mike Boyd laughed out loud. Ms. Beanell swung around and stared at Tiffany.

"What's your name?" she demanded.

Would you believe Marilyn Monroe? Tiffany thought to herself. "Tiffany Larson," she then admitted.

"Tiffany Larson," Ms. Beanell said. "I'm disappointed in you. You're old enough to know how to act in a library."

Ms. Beanell told the other students that they were free for the rest of the hour to look around the library. But Tiffany had to sit at the computer table. *What's wrong?* Tiffany kept asking herself. *I was just being funny!*

When Ms. Carver came to get the class, she talked quietly for a minute with the librarian. Ms. Carver glanced over at Tiffany and nodded.

* * * * * * * * * *

That evening at home, Tiffany did a comedy skit for her parents after dinner. "This is what a goldfish looks like when he needs glasses," said Tiffany. She bulged her eyes, puckered her lips, and wiggled her fingers. It was the same face she'd made behind Ms. Beanell's back.

"Oh, Tiff!" exclaimed Mrs. Larson. "That's perfect! It's the goofiest goldfish I've ever seen!"

Tiffany smiled. Her parents were cracking up at the same jokes that made the librarian angry. It just proved that some adults had a sense of humor and others didn't!

"Do you think I'll get the starring role in the class play?" Tiffany asked.

"I hope so, honey," answered her mother.

"Don't be disappointed if you don't get the lead part," her dad added. "Just do your best and have fun."

What's wrong, Tiffany wondered. *Don't they think I can get the princess role? I'll show them I can do it and make them really proud of me!*

Later that evening, Tiffany walked into Carol's room. It was strange to be in her sister's room when she was gone. It seemed so empty without her. Tiffany looked at the cheerleading medals on Carol's bookshelf. She glanced over the photographs of Carol in prom dresses beside handsome guys. Then there was the picture she had sent from California. Carol looked tan and pretty, standing on the beach with the family she was staying with.

It's not fair, Tiffany told herself. *It's easy for Carol to make friends. And Carol's always doing something to make people proud of her. Someday I will, too! And the starring role in the play is a big first step toward being the most popular kid in my class!*

That night, before she fell asleep, Tiffany had an idea. "It's perfect!" she cried, sitting straight up. "It's the greatest frog joke ever! And if this doesn't get Ms. Carver's attention nothing will!"

Six

"I'm sorry, but I can't eat lunch with you to-day," Tiffany told Erin and Heather the next day when the lunch bell rang.

"You're not going to go eat some more bugs, are you?" Erin asked.

"Don't worry," Tiffany answered. "I'm not going to go eat anything."

"What do you think she means by that?" Heather asked.

"I don't know," said Erin. "But something tells me it's going to be interesting."

Tiffany just smiled and said nothing. Then she turned and disappeared down the hall. She ran up the stairway, then paused outside Mr. Stickney's science classroom. After looking up and down the hall, she opened the door and slipped in.

* * * * * * * * * *

When the bell ending lunch rang, Tiffany's heart began to pound. She ran to her desk in the science room when she heard the sound of students' footsteps in the hall. The door opened and the kids took their seats.

Mr. Stickney appeared in a white lab coat. He straightened his glasses and said, "Good afternoon, class. Today we're going to study the jumping response of frogs."

He reached under a lab table. Then he scratched his chin. "That's funny," he muttered. "I know I put the frog cage under this table."

Mr. Stickney turned to the class. He said, "Students, you'll need paper and pencil to take notes." He peered under the table again, murmuring, "Now where did they disappear to?"

A sudden scream broke the quiet of the room,

70

then another scream and another as the students reached into their desks.

"Oooooo!" squealed Heather. "I touched it!"

"What is it?" shrieked Allison.

"It's slimy! And green!" Arlene screamed.

"Hey!" Mike Boyd yelled. "There's a frog in my desk!"

Suddenly, the classroom was filled with hopping, croaking frogs. Kids jumped away from their desks. Chairs clattered to the floor. Everyone was screaming, except the frogs. And they were croaking.

"Class! Class!" shouted Mr. Stickney. "Settle down!"

Large green frogs jumped from desks to chairs to the floor. They hopped and croaked and jumped and burped their froggy noises. Bulging froggy eyes stared from desktops and shelves. Teachers from the classrooms around the science lab popped in the door to see what was going on. It was total madness!

"Careful! Don't step on them!" yelled Mr.

Stickney above the screaming.

Tiffany had never felt so excited in her life. This was the greatest joke of all time! The science lab was like a huge pot of frog soup!

Erin shot Tiffany a glance. "Now I know what you were doing during lunch hour!" she hissed.

"Catch them! Catch them!" Mr. Stickney yelled.

It took almost another half-hour before the frogs were back in their cage. Four were still missing when Mr. Stickney stood in front of the class. He wiped a drop of sweat from under his nose. Then he sniffed at his finger. *His hand must smell pretty darn froggy*, Tiffany thought.

The teacher with the froggy fingers stared at the classroom. He looked almost too mad to talk. Taking a deep breath, he said, "I want to know right now who did this. Who let the frogs go?"

Tiffany felt her stomach sink into her shoes. She didn't dare breathe. She watched Mr. Stickney's angry, red face.

"Who did this?" he repeated.

Don't anybody look at me, Tiffany thought. *Don't snitch on me. No one knows I did it, do they?*

But Tiffany felt her face getting hot. All the kids had turned to look at her. *How do they all know it's me?* she wondered.

Mr. Stickney stared straight at Tiffany. The room was silent. "Tiffany Larson," he said, "Did you let the frogs out?"

Tiffany was tempted to tell him she didn't do it. *They can never prove it was me*, she told herself. But instead she answered in a quiet voice, "It was just a joke. It was for the class play—*Frog Soup*. Don't you understand?"

"A joke?" Mr. Stickney said. "A joke? We've wasted the whole class period, we've disturbed all the classes around us, and we've lost four frogs!"

"CRRRROOAAKKK!"

Mike raised his hand and said, "Only three, Mr. Stickney. Here's another one." He reached under a bookshelf and pulled out a squirming,

74

wriggling frog. As he walked up to the front of the class to put the frog in the cage, all the students giggled some more.

"No talking for the rest of class!" shouted Mr. Stickney. Tiffany heard quiet laughter from somewhere in the room.

"Not one peep!" Mr. Stickney repeated.

But the sound of laughter cheered Tiffany up. It seemed as if the kids loved her frog joke, even if Mr. Stickney didn't think it was very funny. From around the room, Tiffany heard students trying their hardest to hide their giggles.

Mr. Stickney sat down at his desk and wrote on a piece of paper. He folded the paper and put it into an envelope. Tiffany froze as he walked to her desk. He handed her the letter and said "Give this to your parents, young lady."

When the bell rang, the students left the science room. When they were in the hallway, Tiffany felt hands reach out and pat her on the back.

"Way to go!"

"Great joke!"

"I've never seen so many frogs in my life!"

"Wait until I write to Gina Gold and tell her about this!"

Tiffany felt her confidence returning. All her classmates seemed to think she was the funniest kid ever! She couldn't help grinning. Her plan was working perfectly. She felt that the role of the frog princess was already hers. Whom else could they give it to? Nobody was as crazy as she was. Not even Gina Gold!

But then Tiffany remembered the envelope in her pocket. *Hmm, that might be a problem*, she decided. She took it out, opened the envelope, and read the letter:

> *Dear Mr. and Mrs. Larson,*
> *It is my unpleasant duty to inform you that your daughter Tiffany has become a disruptive influence in my science class. I would appreciate it if you would call me so that we can discuss this matter.*

Sincerely,

Mr. Edgar Stickney

Tiffany felt her heart drum faster as she read the note. Why didn't teachers have a sense of humor? Why can't they take a joke?

She was staring at the letter in the hallway when she felt another tap on her shoulder. She looked up to see Ben Poston, one of the most popular guys in her science class.

"What a fantastic joke!" he exclaimed. "Did you see Mr. Stickney's face when that frog landed on his shoe?"

Tiffany smiled in spite of the letter in her hand. She didn't even know Ben. And here he was telling her that her joke was fantastic. It sure looked as if pulling pranks was the way to make friends!

Ben walked with Tiffany to her next class. She couldn't help noticing that some of the kids she and Ben passed in the hall were looking at her in a different way. *They all know who I am now,* she told herself. *If I keep this up, I'll be even more popular than Carol!*

As she and Ben passed a trash can in the hall, Tiffany wadded up the letter from Mr. Stickney and tossed it in.

Seven

Tiffany felt like a movie star on Monday morning. As she walked down the hallway, she heard students talking around her.

"That's the girl who ate the bugs!"

"She was the dying Indian at the pep rally!"

"She tried out for the boys' football team!"

"Her name's Tiffany Larson. She let all the frogs loose in the science lab!"

"Have you seen her imitate the librarian?"

Tiffany couldn't help smiling. *Who are all the kids talking about? Me! Being popular is great!* she decided. *There's nothing like it.*

"Hurry up, Tiff. We'll be late for English!" Erin grabbed Tiffany's elbow, and they raced down the hall to English class. As Tiffany took her seat, she saw Ms. Carver standing in front of the class. Tiffany smiled. Then she glanced at the sign-up sheet for *Frog Soup* on the bulletin board.

Only a few days until the tryouts, worried Tiffany, *and Ms. Carver hasn't said a thing about all the crazy things I've done. She must have heard about the frogs and the football team.*

Erin leaned across the aisle and whispered, "Tiff! Are you going to the dance in the gym after school before the sixth-grade football game?"

"You bet!" said Tiffany. "Mom said I could go."

"It's really going to be neat," said Erin. "I'm a little scared, though. The seventh and eighth-graders will be there!"

"Let's go together!" suggested Tiffany.

Ms. Carver had the class write dialogues. Tiffany decided to write a funny one to show the teacher how many jokes she knew. Tiffany wrote:

Betty: "Does your dog have a license?"

Frank: "No. He's not old enough to drive."

Betty: "What's wrong with your dog's face? He doesn't have a nose! How does he smell?"

Frank: "Just awful!"

When the bell rang, Tiffany signed her name on her paper extra large and turned it in. She and Erin hurried to their next class, which was math. Ms. Herminghausen, the math teacher, waved a piece of chalk and asked, "If you have three nickels, a dime, six pennies, and five quarters in your pocket, what would you have?

"Someone else's pants!" Tiffany called out.

The class roared. Ms. Herminghausen frowned.

"Knock! Knock!" Tiffany said loudly.

"Who's there?" Keith Johnson answered.

"Olive."

"Olive who?"

"Olive here, so get away from my house!" answered Tiffany.

The whole class laughed again. Kids stamped their feet on the floor.

"Class!" shouted Ms. Herminghausen.

"That's enough! Settle down!" Then she wrote Tiffany's name on the blackboard, along with several others.

"Tiffany, Allison, Arlene, and Keith, you'll report to detention today during study hall," ordered Ms. Herminghausen.

Tiffany slumped in her seat. It seemed as if all she did lately was get into trouble. *What's wrong with teachers?* Tiffany wondered. *Why can't they take a joke? I'm sure glad the kids like my jokes.*

At the end of the day, Tiffany joined Erin by her locker. "How was detention?" Erin asked.

"It was okay."

Erin looked serious for a second. "Maybe you shouldn't keep trying to be funny all the time," she said.

"Why? You know how much it means for me to get the lead role in the play. I've told you a million times."

"I know," answered Erin. "But sometimes I think getting in trouble with the teachers isn't the best way to show them you deserve the best role."

Tiffany slammed her locker shut. "It's not my fault if teachers don't have a sense of humor. At least the kids like me. They all think I'm funnier than Gina Gold."

Erin shrugged her shoulders.

"Come on," Tiffany said. "Let's go to the dance."

When Tiffany and Erin got to the gym, they saw that most of their friends in the sixth grade were huddled by the bleachers. Seventh and eighth-graders were in other parts of the gym.

"I feel like we're the babies of the school," Tiffany said. She looked around at the decorations and saw a stereo on a table. Zack Olson, an eighth-grader, stood behind the table with a microphone in his hand.

"For our first song, I'm going to play a fast number for all you Madison Bulldog fans!" His voice boomed through the gym. Loud music blared from the speakers. Some of the older kids began to dance on the gym floor. But the sixth-graders stayed in their corner looking at one another.

"The sixth-graders are too scared to dance," whispered Erin.

Tiffany looked around at the other sixth-graders sitting nervously in the bleachers. *Maybe this is another chance to let everyone know who I am,* she thought.

"Where are you going?" asked Erin.

"I'm going to show the older kids that we're not all scaredy-cats!" Tiffany shouted above the music.

With a crazy yell, she raced onto the middle of the gym floor. She took a deep breath and tried to make her knees stop shaking. She felt all the kids in the gym staring at her. "I'd better get used to this if I'm going to be a star," she muttered to herself.

Tiffany tapped her feet against the floor. She found herself moving across the gym floor in a wild, hopping dance. The other dancers stopped and stared at her. First, there was laughter from the bleachers. Then, one by one, other sixth-graders crept slowly out onto the dance floor and joined her.

When the song ended, Tiffany was standing by the table with Zack. "Here you go, *Hot Shot*," he said, handing the microphone to Tiffany.

Tiffany took the microphone as if it was a stick of dynamite. Hundreds of eyes gaped at her.

"Uhh...uhhh"

She had no idea what to say. But she knew she had to say something. Suddenly she had an idea. She started cheering, "Go Bulldogs! Beat the Pirates!"

The other students cheered with her and clapped along. Tiffany noticed that even the older kids joined in. Zack Olson stepped aside with a smile. He let Tiffany keep the microphone.

She suddenly felt like a comedian in a night-club or on TV. "Hey, what do you get if you cross a robber with a cement mixer?" she asked.

When no answer came, she shouted, "A hardened criminal!" and slapped her thigh.

Laughter poured from the dance floor and the bleachers, where most of the sixth-graders were now sitting. Tiffany smiled as she looked across the crowd. But she almost fainted when she looked over toward the back wall. It was Ms. Carver! Ms. Carver had a smile on her face.

Tiffany felt her heart pound. *Now's my big chance to prove to Ms. Carver that I'd be perfect for the class play!* she told herself. *Don't blow it!*

Taking a deep breath, Tiffany began again. Her voice sounded awfully loud.

"Why aren't elephants allowed on the beach?" Tiffany asked.

"Why?" someone shouted.

"Because their trunks might fall down!"

The sixth-graders laughed loudly and stamped their feet against the bleachers. It sounded like thunder. Tiffany noticed Keith Johnson standing nearby.

"Where's the driest place to stand in a rainstorm?" Tiffany asked the crowd.

"Where?"

"Under Keith Johnson's nose!" Tiffany yelled.

The bleachers erupted in laughter as everyone turned to look at Keith Johnson. He touched his nose and looked embarrassed.

"What has four eyes and flies?" asked Tiffany.

"What?" the crowd yelled.

"Arlene Dobbs when she doesn't take a bath!"

All faces turned to stare at Arlene. Her eyes looked big behind her glasses, and her face blushed a bright pink.

Tiffany walked close to the bleachers with the microphone in her hand, like a comedian walking out into the crowd. Looking over the crowd, she kept picking out classmates to tell jokes on.

"Hey, Mike!" Tiffany called, pointing at Mike Boyd. "Is that your head, or is your neck blowing bubbles?"

There was more laughter. Several paper airplanes sailed in the direction of Mike's head. Pointing a finger, Tiffany said, "Yo, Erin! Want to hide twenty pounds of ugly fat? Put a paper bag

over your head!"

Tiffany knew she was on a roll and couldn't stop. "Do you know what can knock a buzzard off a dump truck?" she asked. "Heather Truman's breath!"

After she had picked out a dozen more kids to tell jokes on, Tiffany finally said, "Thanks. You've been a great audience. I accept cash, checks, and credit cards!"

Tiffany handed the microphone back to Zack Olson. "Way to go, Squirt," he said and went to play some more records.

Before Tiffany went to sit with her friends, she turned to see if Ms. Carver was still in the gym. Tiffany just saw the English teacher disappear through the door. *Fantastic!* she thought. *Ms. Carver heard the whole thing. Frog princess, here I come!*

Tiffany walked across the floor and climbed up into the bleachers. Still floating on a cloud from being the star, she sat down beside Erin.

"Wasn't I great?" Tiffany said. "I can't believe

I had the guts to tell all those jokes. Hey, it's almost time for the football game. Want to go with me?"

Erin looked down at her feet. "Uhh, no, Tiff," she said. "I'm going with Arlene and Heather."

Eight

T he next morning began mostly in the usual way. Tiffany waited by her locker for Erin. But Erin never came. *Maybe she's sick,* Tiffany thought. But when she got to English class, Erin was already at her desk. Erin was holding a white envelope in her hand. When Tiffany came into the room, Erin quickly tried to put the envelope in her notebook.

"Hey, what's that?" asked Tiffany, pointing at the envelope.

Erin looked embarrassed. "Umm, it's an invitation," she explained quietly.

"An invitation to what?" Tiffany asked.

"Well, Heather's having a party after the fall play," said Erin. Her eyes darted this way and

91

that way, as if she couldn't look Tiffany in the face. Tiffany felt an awful sinking feeling in her stomach.

Then Ms. Carver stood in front of the class. "Remember! Tryouts for *Frog Soup* are next Monday," she announced. "Just a few more days!"

Tiffany tried to get excited about the tryouts. But she couldn't stop wondering why her best friend was treating her as if she had the chicken pox. And what was going on with that invitation? *I know,* she told herself. *Heather's invitation is in my locker! I just didn't notice it. Maybe it fell behind a book.*

When English class was over, Tiffany raced to her locker. She clawed through the books, papers and gym shoes at the bottom. She looked everywhere for the little, white invitation. But it wasn't there. As Tiffany stared into her locker, she overheard three kids walking behind her in the hallway.

"Are you going to Heather's party after the

play?" asked one. "Me, too! Everyone's invited!"

"I heard she hired a magician!"

"I'm going to wear my red velvet dress. What are you going to wear?"

"Do you think Jeren Lukens will ask me to dance? I'll faint if he does!"

Tiffany stood quietly at her locker, listening as the kids walked by. She felt as if she were invisible. *What's going on?* she thought as her lower lip started to tremble. *What's wrong with me? Am I the only one not invited to Heather's party?*

She turned her head quickly when she heard a kid say, "Look! That's the girl who eats bugs."

"Didn't she try out for the boys' football team?" the other student asked.

They think I'm funny, Tiffany thought bitterly. But somehow it wasn't enough anymore. *There must be something more to becoming popular than having a reputation for eating bugs*, Tiffany told herself as she walked slowly down the hall.

When she ducked into the girls' bathroom, she found Erin combing her hair in front of a mirror. But when Erin saw Tiffany, she looked embarrassed. Erin pushed her comb into her purse and turned to leave.

"Wait!" Tiffany called.

"I'm going to be late for class," she said.

Tiffany rushed over to face Erin. "What's going on?" she asked. "Why didn't I get invited to Heather's party? And why won't you talk to me? Please tell me, Erin."

Erin looked at Tiffany. She pressed her lips together, without saying a word.

"Please tell me!" begged Tiffany. "Did I do something?"

Erin slowly nodded her head. "People are mad at you, Tiff," she said. "I'm mad at you, too."

Tiffany listened, wide-eyed. "Why?" she asked breathlessly.

Erin shook her head. "Can't you figure it out yourself?"

"No, I don't have any idea!"

Erin started counting on her fingers. "Wendy Hall is mad because you were goofing around at football tryouts. Mike and Heather are mad because they think you wrecked the skit at the pep rally. And then you got Heather, Allison, Arlene, and Keith in trouble in math class. They all got detention!"

Tiffany felt as if her heart were frozen. And Erin was about to run out of fingers to count on. It was an awful feeling to listen to her best friend list all the people who were angry with her.

"Mike, Keith, Heather, Arlene and about half the kids in our grade are mad because you embarrassed them at the dance yesterday. You told all the older kids that Heather's breath could knock a buzzard off a dump truck! That's why she didn't invite you to her party. That and the pep rally."

Tiffany's shoulders slumped.

"And...and...I'm mad because you made everyone laugh at me in the gym yesterday. You practically told everyone I was ugly. Why should I put a bag over my head? I never thought I was that ugly!"

"Gosh! It was just a joke!" Tiffany exclaimed. "Didn't you hear everyone laughing? It was funny!"

"Maybe it was funny for you. But it was embarrassing for me," Erin said. "And for everyone else you told jokes about."

Tiffany felt as if her heart were turning to concrete as she stared at her best friend. She saw the hurt in Erin's eyes for the first time.

"It seems like ever since you decided to try out for *Frog Soup*," Erin said, "you've been acting like a total jerk."

Tiffany didn't know what to say. She hadn't meant to hurt all those people, to make everyone mad at her. She was just trying to be funny so that she could get to be in the play! The worst feeling of all was knowing that she'd hurt her best friend.

Tiffany and Erin walked silently together to math class. Just as Tiffany walked in the door, she heard someone saying, "What do you get when you cross a drill with Tiffany Larson?"

"Boring jokes," someone replied, and quiet laughter rippled through the room.

Tiffany stared at her feet as she walked to her desk. But from the corner of her eye, she saw a little, white envelope sticking out of almost everyone's book or pocket.

The rest of the school day crept by. Tiffany could tell that her friends were ignoring her. At the end of the long day, Tiffany waited by her locker for Erin. She stared anxiously into the crowd of students. But Erin was nowhere in sight. Tiffany walked down the hall alone.

"That's the girl who ate two bugs!" someone whispered.

"She does a great imitation of the librarian!"

"That's Tiffany Larson! She's always telling jokes! She's really funny!"

"Big deal," Tiffany muttered under her breath. "I'd eat a thousand bugs just to have my friends like me again!"

Tiffany walked home alone. Everyone she passed was laughing or talking. Everyone was with someone. Everyone belonged to a group or had a friend. Everyone but her.

Tiffany went straight to her room and closed the door. She flopped onto her bed and stared up at the ceiling through her tears. *How did things ever get so messed up?* she asked herself. *I was only trying to be popular and funny. Now I'm the most unpopular girl in the class! If only Carol were here to talk to. She'd know what I should do. She has loads of friends. But she's so far away...*

Tiffany jumped up when she heard a knock at her door. She dried her eyes and opened the door. She was surprised to see both her parents step into her room. Her dad held a piece of paper and looked very serious.

"What's wrong?" asked Tiffany. It didn't seem possible that life could get any worse than it already was. But the looks on her parents' faces told her that something was wrong—really wrong.

"We just received this letter from your science teacher," her dad said.

Oh no! Tiffany had forgotten all about the letter from Mr. Stickney!

"He says that he sent a note home with you from school," her dad went on. "He says that you were supposed to give us that note."

Tiffany sat speechless on the edge of her bed. Her stomach turned a flip-flop as she remembered the letter for her parents that she had dropped into the trash can at school.

"Oh, Tiffany! Did you really put frogs in the desks at school?" her mother asked. "Did you really disrupt the class?"

Tiffany nodded her head and stared down at the floor.

"We're very disappointed in you, young lady," her dad said.

Tiffany looked up meekly at her parents. "It was supposed to be a joke," she said. "I only wanted to be funny."

Neither of her parents smiled. "Not all jokes

are funny," her dad said. Tiffany started to cry again.

Her dad sat down on the bed next to her and put his arm around her. "I'm sure you didn't mean to hurt anyone," he said gently. "But joking around at the wrong time and in the wrong place can get you into big trouble, as you found out."

Tiffany sniffed. "Oh, Dad, it's even worse than you think," Tiffany answered between sniffs. Then she told them all about her friends being mad at her and not getting invited to Heather's party.

"I think everything will work out if you just give it time," her mother said after she had heard the whole story. "You've learned a tough lesson about how to be a friend."

"There's nothing wrong with being funny," added her father. "But you have to be sure you're not hurting people."

"I know that now, believe me," Tiffany sniffed.

"We'll think about how you ought to be punished for this frog business," her mom said.

After her parents left her alone, Tiffany lay on her bed, hugging a pillow. "What do you get when you mix a loser with bad jokes and a bunch of frogs?" she asked herself.

A big tear plopped onto the pillow as Tiffany answered her own riddle. "You get a geek with no friends," she whispered. "Me."

Nine

Tiffany cried herself to sleep. And the next morning, she walked into the school alone. When she passed Erin and Heather in the hall, she looked at them hopefully. But neither girl said hi to her.

The only thing left to look forward to is getting the best role in the class play, she told herself sadly. *But even that will be ultra-weird when everyone else in the play goes to Heather's party and I don't!*

"Hello, Tiffany."

Tiffany looked up in surprise to see the friendly face of Ms. Carver. "Are you ready for play tryouts on Monday?" the English teacher asked.

Tiffany nodded. "I sure am!" she exclaimed.

"Good," Ms. Carver answered. "I'm glad you're trying out."

Tiffany decided that tryouts for *Frog Soup* were more important than ever, now that everyone was mad at her. She remembered what her mom had said, that being the star of the play gave her confidence and helped her make new friends. *I could sure use some of both*, Tiffany thought.

Tiffany followed her teacher into English class. She was happy and relieved to know that at least one person in the state of Kansas was still talking to her!

The rest of the day dragged on. Tiffany walked to her classes alone. She brushed her hair in the bathroom alone, without the usual crowd of giggling girls around her. She ate lunch in the cafeteria alone. Breathing into her hand, Tiffany muttered, "My breath smells okay. I guess it's my personality that stinks."

Walking home alone after school, Tiffany daydreamed about what she could do. "I wonder if Mom and Dad would let me go live in Utah with Aunt Jean. Nobody hates me in Utah—not yet, anyway."

When she walked into her house, her mother called, "Tiffany! Is that you? Come here for a minute!"

Oh, no! Am I in trouble again? Tiffany wondered. She found her mother in the kitchen.

"There's a letter from Carol. I put it in your room on the dresser!" her mother said. "She says she won her first debate!"

Tiffany tried to feel happy. She made herself smile and said, "That's great, Mom. Well, I've got homework to do."

Tiffany left the kitchen and walked to her bedroom. She picked up Carol's letter from the dresser. *I'm too depressed to read it*, she decided.

"I'm the most unpopular girl in Madison...in Kansas...in the United States...on the planet Earth," she whispered. "Face it, I'm the biggest dweeb in the whole universe!"

Lying on her bed, she wished there were

someone she could talk to. "I could call Erin," she said to herself. "But she's mad at me. So is Heather. Mike Boyd's mad, too. And so are Arlene, Allison, and Susie. And even if I wanted to, I couldn't call up Mr. Stickney or Ms. Beanell. They don't like me either!"

But the worst was Erin. They had been best friends for years. She remembered how Erin had always stuck by her. Erin was beside her when they first walked into the strange, new school. Erin had been there when Tiffany ate the giant beetles. She had watched Tiffany try out for the boys' football team. And Erin never told on her when Tiffany made fun of the librarian behind her back, or when she let the frogs loose in science class.

But now Erin was hurt, and it was all because of Tiffany's joke. "How could I have been so stupid," Tiffany wondered. "I should have known they all would have been hurt. I never should have made fun of all my friends like that."

Tiffany remembered the hurt look in Erin's

eyes. *What can I do to get my friends back?* she groaned. *Who can I talk to?*

She opened the envelope in her hand. She skimmed over Carol's letter. She caught her breath as she read the last line:

P.S. If you ever need to talk to someone, call me!

Tiffany hopped up and ran to the kitchen. "Mom! Mom! Can I call Carol?" she asked.

Mrs. Larson looked at Tiffany. "Well, sure," she said. "Go ahead. I think this is the day she comes home early from school."

Tiffany ran to her parents' bedroom and dialed the telephone. "Please be there," she whispered. "Please be there!"

"Hello?" It was Carol's voice!

"Hi," said Tiffany. "It's me!"

"What's wrong?" asked Carol. "You sound upset."

Tiffany sniffed. It felt good to talk with the one

person in the world who could tell how she felt, even from hundreds of miles away.

"I'm in trouble," Tiffany said in a choking voice. "Everyone hates me!"

The whole story came pouring out. Tiffany told her sister about all the pranks, from football to frogs. "I only did it because I wanted to be popular," she said, "like you! Everyone loves you! You're good at everything! You never have any problems!"

Carol sighed. "Listen, Tiff, " she said. "I used to worry about being popular, just like you. Did you know that I gave away all my toys in third grade? I gave them to all the neighborhood kids just so that they'd like me."

"You did?" Tiffany asked. "I didn't know that. What happened?"

Carol laughed. "I didn't have enough toys for all the kids," she said. "So the ones who didn't get toys were mad at me. And Mom and Dad were mad," she admitted. "Here I was giving all my stuff away! You should have seen them when

they found out!"

Tiffany smiled a little. It was hard to think of her older, beautiful, popular sister trying so hard to get people to like her.

"I learned something from that, Tiff," Carol continued. "I learned that not everyone is always going to like me. No matter what I do, I can't please everyone. So I just try to be as nice as I can. And if they like me, then that's fine. And if they don't like me...well, maybe they will someday. But I'm just not going to worry about it now. You know what I think the most important thing is?"

"What is it, Carol?" Tiffany asked.

"I try to be the sort of person that my friends can trust," Carol said. "I don't put them down or hurt their feelings. The way to be popular is to be a good friend."

Tiffany squirmed. "I guess I haven't exactly been a very good friend," she admitted. "I hurt a lot of people's feelings."

Suddenly Tiffany sat straight up. "I know!" she exclaimed. "Carol, I'll apologize to everyone.

I'll think of a funny way to do it so that they won't be mad anymore! Maybe I'll send everyone a telegram! Or I can drop letters from a hot air balloon! That would be a riot!"

"Uhh, Tiff. Didn't joking around get you into this mess in the first place?" asked Carol.

Tiffany was quiet for a second. "Yeah," she admitted. "I guess you're right. Maybe I'll just call everyone on the phone and apologize."

Tiffany felt a knot growing in her stomach as she thought about calling all the people she'd hurt. "It'll be embarrassing to apologize," she said.

"I know it will," Carol said. "But it's the right thing to do. You can do it, Tiff. You're smart and funny. You're strong and nice."

"I am?" asked Tiffany.

"Sure you are!" said Carol. "I wouldn't have just anybody for a sister, would I?"

Tiffany laughed. Then she said, "I miss you, Carol. I wish you could come home. It seems like forever since you were home."

"I miss you, too," Carol answered.

"Thanks for listening."

"Hang in there. You'll be okay," said Carol. "Be sure to let me know how it all works out."

When Tiffany hung up the phone, she felt how much she missed her sister. How could she ever wait until the end of the school year to see her?

She took a deep breath and stared at the telephone. Then she dialed Erin's number. Tiffany gulped when she heard Erin's voice on the other end. Gathering her courage, Tiffany apologized for hurting Erin's feelings.

She sighed with relief when Erin said, "That's okay, Tiff. I accept your apology. I've missed you. But please, promise you won't embarrass me in front of the whole school ever again. Okay?"

"I won't," Tiffany promised.

It took over a half-hour to call all the people on her list, but she got through it. It felt weird to call Mr. Stickney and Ms. Beanell on the phone. It was especially hard to call Heather, knowing that Heather hadn't invited her to her party. But even Heather accepted Tiffany's apology.

At last, there was only one phone call left to make. "Hello, Ms. Carver?" Tiffany said into the phone. "This is Tiffany Larson. I apologize for not following the script at the pep rally. I'm sorry that I didn't behave in the library when you left us there. And I'm sorry I goofed around in the hallway and in class. I guess my jokes sort of got a little out of control."

"It took a lot of courage to call me," the teacher said. "Thanks. And I'll see you at the tryouts, I hope."

"You bet!" Tiffany answered. "Uhh, would it be okay if I told some jokes at the tryouts?"

"Of course, it would," Ms. Carver answered. "There's a right time and a right place for joking. I think a tryout for a comedy is a perfect place for jokes, don't you?"

"Yep!"

When Tiffany hung up the phone, she told

herself, "It's not too late! I can still get the lead role in the play. I'll make Mom and Dad proud of me!"

Visions of frog princesses hopped into Tiffany's mind as she imagined herself on stage in front of the whole school.

"Hollywood, here I come," she whispered.

Ten

When Monday morning finally came, Tiffany discovered a little white envelope inside her locker at school. She tore it open. It was an invitation to Heather's party! Tiffany tucked the invitation into her purse.

"Hi, Tiff!" came a familiar voice behind her. "Are you ready for the tryouts?"

Tiffany whirled around to find Erin standing beside her locker. Seeing her best friend brought a grin to Tiffany's face. "I'm ready!" Tiffany said. "I have some new jokes. I worked on them all weekend!"

"Good luck!" said Erin. "I hope you get the starring role."

A few minutes later when they walked into

English class, they saw a roomful of noisy actors practicing their lines. Mike Boyd wore a frog mask and hopped around the room.

Why didn't I think of wearing a frog mask? Tiffany asked herself.

"Okay, class," said Ms. Carver. "Let's get started. Remember, there are two lead roles, for one girl and one boy. Not everyone can have a starring role. All the parts are important."

Not to me they aren't, Tiffany thought. *I'm going to be the princess!*

One by one the students performed brief skits in front of the class. Tiffany watched as Heather danced and sang. Tiffany tried to push her jealous feelings away. She had to admit that Heather was good—really good.

At last it was Tiffany's turn to face the class. At a nod from Ms. Carver, Tiffany walked to the front of the room. Her heart pounded. She gulped and began her routine.

"How do Martians make coffee?" Tiffany asked the class. When no one answered, she

said, "The Milky Way, of course."

Erin laughed loudly. Tiffany was thankful for her friend's support.

"Why did the one-handed ghost cross the road?" asked Tiffany.

"I don't know," Ms. Carver said. "Why did the one-handed ghost cross the road?"

"To get to the second-hand shop," answered Tiffany.

A burst of giggling and some groans rippled through the room. Tiffany started to feel better. "Do you know why giraffes have long necks?" she asked.

"No. Why?" asked the class.

"Because they have smelly feet!" answered Tiffany with a grin.

She heard the laughter and thought, *They think I'm funny. And I'm not embarrassing any-one!* After a lot more jokes, she bowed and returned to her chair.

When the last student had performed, Ms. Carver said, "You all did a lovely job! It's going to be a hard decision. I'll post the list of cast members on the bulletin board after school."

Students groaned. "Ms. Carver, do we have to wait until school's over to find out?" Tiffany asked.

"Sorry," said the teacher with a smile. "I need the whole day to think about it so that I can make the right decisions. You'll just have to wait."

The day seemed to drag on and on. But at last, the final bell of the day rang. Tiffany raced down the hall to her English classroom. She found a group of squealing students already huddled around the bulletin board. Anxiously, Tiffany pushed through the crowd and stared at the paper on the board. She read Mrs. Carver's choices for the play.

Cast of *Frog Soup*

Frog Prince..Mike Boyd
Frog Princess................................Heather Truman
Star Baby...Arlene Dobbs

Dancing Mushroom........................Tiffany Larson
Forest King..Jeren Lukens
Forest Queen..Allison Bosley
Elf...James Paoletti

"I got it! I got it!" Heather squealed. She jumped up and down, clapping her hands.

Tiffany felt as if her heart were sinking through her stomach, down into her knees, and settling, at last, somewhere in her shoes. "I'm the...dancing mushroom?" she asked. She checked the list once again just to make sure.

Dancing Mushroom........................Tiffany Larson

There it was. She wasn't imagining things. She turned to Heather and Mike. "Congratulations," she said, forcing herself to smile.

She found Erin waiting for her at her locker. Erin tried to cheer her up. "At least you got a part in the play," she said. "Think of all the people who tried out who didn't make it at all."

Tiffany shook her head sadly. "What will Mom and Dad think when they find out I didn't get the starring role?" she asked. "Mom was the best actress in her school. Carol's the smartest girl in her class. They'll think I'm a big loser!"

Tiffany zipped her jacket with a groan and started home. It was a gloomy walk. With her feet dragging the whole way, it took a long time. When she finally walked into her house, Tiffany found her parents sitting in the living room.

Tiffany dropped her books on the floor. "Hi, Mom, hi, Dad. Guess what?"

"What?" her mother asked.

Scowling, Tiffany said, "I'm a mushroom."

Her mother looked puzzled. "You're a what?" she asked.

Tiffany hung her head in disappointment. "I'm a dancing mushroom," she said. "I didn't get the part of the Frog Princess in the class play."

Tiffany's mother crossed the room and hugged Tiffany. "Congratulations, honey!" she said. "That's fantastic! You're in the play!"

Tiffany looked at her mother in surprise. "But I'm not the star," Tiffany said.

Her father came over and put his arm around Tiffany. "That's not what's important at all, Tiff," he said. "We just want you to do the best you can and have fun. We're very proud of you!"

"Even if I'm just a mushroom?" Tiffany asked.

Her mother squeezed Tiffany's hand and said, "You'll be the very best mushroom Madison Middle School ever had!"

"And where did you ever get the idea that we would only be proud of you if you were the star of the play?" her father asked.

"I don't know," Tiffany muttered. "I just thought that since you and Mom were the stars of your play, you'd want me to be the star, too."

"Tiffany Larson!" her mother said. "I hope you realize how dumb that sounds! We love you, and we're proud of you, whether you're the star or not."

"That's right," added her dad. "It doesn't

make any difference at all."

Tiffany felt tears in her eyes. To hear her parents say that they loved her no matter what was even better than being the star of the play!

Tiffany took a deep breath. "You know," she said, "maybe being a mushroom isn't so bad after all!"

Eleven

"I can't believe we've been practicing the play for a month," Tiffany said at the lunch table.

"I know," said Heather. "I never thought I'd be able to memorize all my lines. But I think I've got most of them."

"I remember thinking way back when we started that October would never get here," added Erin, who had decided to work on the stage crew for the play. "Now it's here and the play is next week!"

"I bet this is going to be the best play the sixth grade has ever put on," said Arlene, taking a bite out of her hot dog.

"And I bet your party is going to be the best party ever, too!" Tiffany said to Heather. Everyone at the table agreed.

"I'm helping with the party decorations," Erin said.

"I'm bringing the punch," Arlene said. "It's ginger ale and grape juice."

Mike Boyd grinned. "Heather asked me to bring all of my new CDs and tapes," he said.

"My mom and I have been baking cookies every night this week," said Susie Kurtz.

"Hey, what can I bring?" asked Tiffany. "How about potato chips and dip?"

"Actually," answered Heather, glancing around the table, "everything's taken care of. I can't think of anything that's left to do."

The other kids at the table grew quiet. Tiffany looked from one to the next. But no one met her gaze.

Something's going on, Tiffany told herself. *But what did I do now? Is everyone mad at me again? I've been trying not to embarrass anyone. I haven't let any frogs loose, I haven't goofed on the librarian, and I haven't gotten anyone in trouble. What is it?*

"I've got to go!" said Heather, looking at her watch. She jumped up from the table.

"Me, too!" said Arlene.

"Me, too!" said Susie.

The three girls left the table. They whispered together. With a backward glance at Tiffany, they disappeared through the cafeteria door.

"Erin, what's going on?" asked Tiffany.

"Nothing," said Erin, quietly. She stared down at her plate.

But Tiffany knew something was up. All afternoon she wondered what she could have done to make her friends mad at her again. *Just when I thought everything was going okay!*

Then she reminded herself what Carol had told her about just being nice. *Just be the kind of person your friends can trust*. Thinking about her sister made Tiffany miss her again all the more. *If only Carol could come see me in the play*, she thought sadly. *But California's so far away. It would cost too much to fly home just to see me in a play.*

The last week before the play flew by. There was so much to do, with memorizing lines and finishing up her mushroom costume. But even though Tiffany was busy, two things were on her mind almost the whole time. She wished there were some way Carol could see her in the play. And then, there was the weird way her friends acted toward her.

It wasn't all the time. It was only when they talked about Heather's party. Even Erin got a little strange and quiet. The rest of the time everyone was fine, and they all had a great time together. Tiffany just couldn't figure it out.

* * * * * * * * * *

And then, it was the Friday of the play, the day all the kids had been waiting for. Trying to concentrate in class was hopeless. Tiffany was a nervous wreck.

"I hope I don't throw up on stage," she kept

telling Erin. "Do you think I'll be so nervous that I'll barf?"

Erin laughed. "For the hundredth time," she said, "everything's going to be okay. You're not going to throw up. If you could eat two bugs without barfing, you're not going to throw up over a little play! And you won't forget your lines, either!"

Somehow, Tiffany made it through the day. When she got home, she pulled out her mushroom costume, just to make sure it was perfect. She was in her room smoothing out a tiny wrinkle when she heard her mother calling.

"Tiff, can you set the table?"

"Oh, all right," Tiffany answered. "But I'm so nervous I'll probably drop all the plates."

Down in the kitchen, Tiffany's mom handed her the plates, glasses, and silverware. "I thought it was Dad's turn to set the table," Tiffany said. "Where is he anyway?"

"He'll be here in a minute," her mother answered. "He had to make a stop on the way home from work."

"He won't be late for my play, will he?"

"No way," answered Mrs. Larson. "He wouldn't miss it for the world."

"Oops, Mom," Tiffany said, "you gave me too many plates. We only need three."

"I didn't make a mistake, honey," her mother replied.

"Huh—"

"Oh, there's your dad now."

Tiffany heard the front door open and her father shout, "I'm home!"

Tiffany ran to the door to meet her dad. But he wasn't alone.

Standing next to him, holding a suitcase, was a sun-tanned, smiling Carol!

Tiffany let out a huge squeal of delight and ran to her sister. They hugged for a long time.

"I can't believe you're here!" Tiffany kept saying.

"You didn't think I would miss your first play, did you? I knew I had to come home for the weekend!"

At dinner, Carol told her family about going to school in California. "It's a lot of work," she said. "And it was really hard to make friends at first. All those kids have been going to school with each other since kindergarten. It's tough to break into the groups. But it's going okay. I'm starting to really like it. But I miss everyone back home."

Tiffany was surprised. She had always thought that everything came easy for Carol. But even she had a tough time sometimes. *I guess everyone has problems and worries*, Tiffany decided. *Even my sister Carol. But she doesn't let them get her down. I'll try to remember that.*

"Tiff?" Carol asked in the car on the way to the school. "Remember what I told you about how to make friends? Is it working?"

"I think so," said Tiffany. "The kids at school are talking to me—most of the time. I don't make fun of them anymore. And I haven't put frogs in anyone's desk lately."

When they got to the school, Tiffany left her family in the auditorium. She made her way backstage. The students in the sixth, seventh, and eighth-grade plays were everywhere, whispering and pulling on their costumes. Tiffany found the kids in her play.

"I think there's a herd of wild gerbils running 'round in my stomach," she told Erin. "Can you hear them? I hope I don't bar—"

"Don't say it!" cried Erin with a laugh.

As the starting time for the play got closer, the gerbils in Tiffany's stomach began slam dancing. "I won't barf, I won't barf," she chanted to herself.

A cool hand brushed across Tiffany's neck. "You'll do just fine," said Ms. Carver. She helped Tiffany into her mushroom costume.

Then Ms. Carver disappeared, and the next thing Tiffany knew, Ms. Carver was on the stage announcing the sixth-grade play. Then the velvet curtain rose and the frog prince and frog princess hopped onto the stage. Heather looked pretty, in spite of the big green frog mask she wore.

Tiffany listened carefully for her cue. When she heard it, she skittered onto the stage, taking tiny mushroom steps. "Hello, Prince and Princess," she called loudly. "I'm a dancing mushroom! If you dance with me, you will have good luck forever and ever!"

The play went without a hitch. After the final act, all the players stepped forward to take a bow. From the stage, Tiffany saw her family. Carol waved and clapped like crazy. The curtain fell, and Tiffany breathed a sigh of relief.

"Great job!" Ms. Carver told each person. Tiffany climbed out of her mushroom costume and ran to the girls' bathroom. She changed into a dress for Heather's party. When she left the bathroom, she found Arlene and Susie Kurtz whispering together. They stopped suddenly when they saw Tiffany.

I sure wish I knew what they're always whispering about, Tiffany thought. *But I'm just not going to worry about it anymore!*

Tiffany spotted Erin and hurried over to her. "My parents are dropping me off at Heather's," she said. "Want a ride?"

"No, thanks," said Erin. "I'm going with Arlene and Susie."

"Okay. Well, I'll see you there," Tiffany answered.

It's as if I'm becoming unpopular again, Tiffany thought. *But I know I haven't done anything to make them ignore me.*

Tiffany wondered if maybe she should skip the party and just go home. But for months the kids had talked about how great this party was going to be. She couldn't miss it—not now—not after all the weeks of waiting!

Tiffany felt better when her family came backstage to see her. "You were fantastic!" said her dad proudly.

"We have a real actress in the family," said Carol, hugging her.

In the car on the way to Heather's, Tiffany felt

nervous, as nervous as she had felt before the play. *What if nobody talks to me at the party?* she wondered. *They've all been acting so weird. They might give me the cold shoulder again.*

At least my family loves me, Tiffany reminded herself. *Just like Dad and Mom said—I don't have to be a star for them to love me and be proud of me.*

When they dropped her off at Heather's house, Tiffany's hands were sweaty. Through the window, she saw that many of the kids were already there. They were placing food on a table and putting up decorations. Tiffany took a deep breath and reminded herself that she didn't have to be a star in a play to have confidence. *Confidence comes from doing the very best that you can.*

Tiffany waved goodbye to her family and knocked on the front door.

Tiffany thought she heard giggling. After a while, Heather answered her knock. "Come in, Tiff," said Heather. "We've been waiting for you."

More giggling came from the kids when Tiffany walked in. Everyone seemed to be staring at her.

"Hey, what's going on?" she asked. "Am I still wearing my mushroom costume?"

"Come on in, Tiffany," said Mike Boyd. "There are some great snacks here. We saved some for you. Here."

Mike opened his hand, and Tiffany saw a big, black bug lying in his palm.

"This bug's for you!" he said.

Tiffany wrinkled her nose. "Forget it," she said. "My bug-eating days are over!"

"Oh, come on, Tiffany!" urged Arlene. "Eat a bug!"

When Tiffany looked around the room, she saw that every person was holding a big, black beetle!

Tiffany's stomach turned a somersault. The gross, bitter, buggy taste came back. She shook her head and said, "No, thanks. The doctor said I need to cut down on bugs."

"Well, okay," said Heather, "if that's how you feel. But I hate for good bugs to go to waste. It took Mike a whole day to catch all of these."

Then, as Tiffany watched in horror, Heather popped the beetle into her mouth! Every kid in the room did the same! The sound of 30 bugs being crunched really made Tiffany want to throw up.

"Mmmmmmm, good!" said Heather, chewing her beetle. "Are you sure you won't have one?"

Tiffany shook her head, feeling sicker by the moment. Even Erin was munching the head off of a bug. Tiffany couldn't believe her eyes. She looked closer.

"Wait a minute!" She saw a brown smudge on everyone's hand.

"Those bugs are just chocolate!" screamed Tiffany.

A big grin stretched across Tiffany's face. She looked around the room and saw a sign on the wall that said BUG LOVERS OF AMERICA.

"Since you didn't care for the bugs, come on and look at the other food!" giggled Erin. She led Tiffany to the snack table.

"Care for some bug punch?" asked Mike. A plastic bug floated on top of the ginger ale punch and bobbed up and down as Mike dipped a ladle into the bowl. He handed a cup to Tiffany and she took a sip.

"Mmmmm," she said, "Water bug flavor. How'd you know it was my favorite?"

Tiffany looked across the food table. She saw rubber bugs climbing across the chip dip. Giant plastic flies sat beside the sandwiches. There was even a plate of red and green gummy bugs!

At last Tiffany understood what all the whispering at school had been about. Looking around at all her smiling classmates, she smiled too. "I guess the joke's on me," she said.

Tiffany realized with surprise that every person in the room was her friend. Heather, Mike, Allison, Susie, Arlene, Wendy, Bart, Erin, Keith, and lots more. New friends and old friends.

No way I'm a nobody, she told herself. *Not with all of these good friends. I'm definitely a somebody!*

"Get ready, guys," she announced with a laugh. "I can't resist telling one little joke."

Everyone groaned. Then she asked a riddle. "What's the safest ship to be on in a storm?"

"What?"

"Friend-ship," answered Tiffany. Then she popped a big chocolate bug into her mouth.

About the Author

"I remember what it was like to be a kid," says JANET ADELE BLOSS. "I understand how kids feel things very deeply. And I know that kids love to laugh."

Janet showed signs of becoming an author as early as third grade when she wrote a story entitled "Monkeys on the Moon." By the time Janet reached fifth grade, she had decided to become an author. She also wanted to be a flamenco dancer, a spy, a skater for roller derby, and a beach bum in California. But fortunately for her readers, it was the dream of becoming an author that came true.

"I've always loved books and children," says Janet. "So writing for children is the perfect job for me. It's fun."

Although Janet's first love is writing, her other interests include dancing, music, camping, swimming, ice-skating, and cats.